Everett Anderson's Goodbye

Everett Anderson's Goodbye

by Lucille Clifton
illustrated by
Ann Grifalconi

Henry Holt and Company | New York

Henry Holt and Company, LLC
Publishers since 1866
115 West 18th Street
New York, New York 10011
www.henryholt.com

Henry Holt is a registered trademark of Henry Holt and Company, LLC
Text copyright © 1983 by Lucille Clifton
Illustrations copyright © 1983 by Ann Grifalconi
All rights reserved.
Distributed in Canada by H. B. Fenn and Company Ltd.

Library of Congress Cataloging-in-Publication Data
Clifton, Lucille.
Everett Anderson's goodbye.
Summary: Everett Anderson has a difficult time coming
to terms with his grief after his father dies.
[1. Stories in rhyme. 2. Death—Fiction. 3. Fathers and sons—Fiction.]
I. Grifalconi, Ann, ill. II. Title.
PZ8.3.C573Evh   1983 [E]   82-23426

ISBN 0-8050-0235-9 (hardcover)
20 19 18 17 16 15 14 13
ISBN 0-8050-0800-4 (paperback)
20 19 18 17 16 15

First published in hardcover in 1983 by Holt, Rinehart and Winston
First Owlet paperback edition—1988
Printed in Mexico

for my sad friends

1 Denial
2 Anger
3 Bargaining
4 Depression
5 Acceptance

The Five Stages of Grief

1

Everett Anderson holds the hand
of his mama until he falls asleep
and dreams about Daddy
in his chair, and
at the park, and
everywhere.
Daddy always laughing or never,
just Daddy, Daddy, forever and ever.

2

"I don't love Baby Evelyn
  and I don't love Mr. Perry, too,
  and I don't love Christmas or
  Santa Claus
  and I don't love candy
  and I don't love you!"

"Well, Everett," his mama sighs,
"who do you love?"

And he cries and cries.

3

"I promise to learn my
  nine times nine
  and never sleep late or
  gobble my bread
  if I can see Daddy
  walking, and talking, and
  waving his hand, and
  turning his head.

"I will do everything you say
  if Daddy can be alive today."

Everett Anderson tries to sleep
but it is too hard and
the hurt is too deep.

Everett Anderson likes his food
but how can a dinner
do any good?

Everett Anderson just sits staring,
wondering what's the use of caring.

5

After a little bit of time

Everett Anderson says, "I knew
my daddy loved me through and through,
and whatever happens when people die,

love doesn't stop, and
neither will I."